CAN ANYTHING GOOD COME OUT THE HOOD?

CAN ANYTHING GOOD COME OUT THE HOOD?

BY

TYRE' GADSDEN

SBPC

SIMMS BOOKS PUBLISHING CORPORATION

SBPC

SIMMS BOOKS PUBLISHING CORP.

Publishers Since 2012

Published by Simms Books Publishing Corporation

Jonesboro, GA

Library of Congress Cataloging in Publication Data

2018949715

Tyre' Gadsden

CAN ANYTHING GOOD COME OUT THE HOOD?

ISBN:9780998331171

Printed in the United States of America

Book Arrangement by Simms Books Publishing

Edited by Jeirnear Barr

Proofread by Kasheria Worthy

λ DEDICATION λ

There are no words to describe the hurt of losing a child. There can be no words spoken to explain the pain. I dedicate this book to my son Jacob 'JC' Wright. You are never forgotten, and you are greatly missed. I miss your smile, your laughter and teddy bear hugs. So, we should always cherish every moment we spend with our loved ones. Never let a day go by without telling them that you love them. Because who knows today may just be our last. Thanks to my family and friends for been there for me through such a difficult time. A special thanks to James Simms and Simms Books Publishing Corporation for believing in me and helping to make this book possible!

λ INTRODUCTION λ

So what can I tell you about South Aiken Park? Well, one thing for sure it's no ordinary park or playground. Here is where I grew up and as a young boy this is what I've known all of my life. It was simple, if you were from The Aiken, nobody messed with you. People didn't want their kids out here after dark. Hell, even the cops were afraid to come out here.

After the sun goes down, it's a whole different world. The only people you see then were the drug dealers, and crack heads. Then of cause the girls out here that are doing whatever for some drugs or crack, and then you have the badass wannabe. You have to be careful out here causes this place ain't no joke. I've seen a lot of things just to be 18, probably more than I should but that's life in The Aiken.

My baby Tiffany is smart and fine as hell. Her and Keyna are completely opposite but have been friends since that day some girl tried to bully Tiffany. Boy, Keyna beat that girl down so bad that no one messed with Tiffany ever since. Keyna definitely has issues. Tiffany's mom spends a lot of time at work and church. Ms. Alston is very spiritual. Which is good cause God knows that Keyna needs all the prayers she can get!

Mr. Thomas is some older dude that comes out here every day since I can remember. He always seems to wear the same 3 outfits over and over again, but I can't say he ever smelt bad. He talks a lot of trash about how he could beat somebody, but I have never seen him fight a day in my life. Most all the time you will find him sitting on the bench telling whoever would listen about his time in the war.

He would talk about the *Good Old Days* and how much the park has changed from when he first moved here. He always seems to be concern about us and especially Keyna for some reason. He's always fussing wanting to know when is she going back to school and dumping that deadbeat, want-a-be, non- rapping, so call baby's daddy, Kevin.

Now Sean, that's my boy! We've been friends since he moved here from DC. His mom passed away, so his dad sent him to live with his grandmother. Saying something about his dad wanting to get him away from the city. Little did he know The Aiken was no better. I ran into Sean at school. Well, it was more like he ran into me while some kids were chasing him. Me, my name's Quentin but my friends call me Q and up until now school was a joke, my whole *life* was a joke. Everyone knew me as the class clown. Mrs. Bratton would remind me that time was passing *but* I wasn't.

But me and my boy Sean got plans when we get out of here. I can't wait to check out some other places other than Jacksonville. My Uncle Van had like 13 kids and all of them were bad as hell. Yeah, like going there was a lot of fun! But we're going to Georgia Tech! That's right, you heard me. I said Georgia Tech as in Atlanta Georgia, as in away from this place and I promise I'm never looking back once I leave. I just got to get out of here!

λ WELCOME TO THE AIKEN λ

CHAPTER 1

Aiken Park was cool cause here was where I could meet up with my boys. We would spend hours out here just playing some basketball. But you better watch your mouth with all that cursing! Mr. Thomas will stop you and give you a whole sermon about how disrespectful kids are these days. Everyone here knew Mr. Thomas. Me, myself, I think he's a little mental with some of the things he be saying. I would just listen and agree to *whatever* he says.

"You know what I'm talking about Young Blood?"

Mr. Thomas has told me this story a hundred times about how he uses to bring his daughter out here to play.

"Yes, Sir."

I just kept nodding my head agreeing with him. Sometimes Mr. Thomas would stop talking in the middle of a sentence and just look really sad man. I think he be missing his daughter or something but I'm not sure and too afraid to ask.

"That's one thing I can say about you Quentin, your Momma taught you manners but not these churn out here."

I could hear the voice of a young guy rapping along with Drake on his phone.

"Listening to that loud noise, can't understand half of what they saying anyway. You know that rapper Flocka aka, Maka Flocka. You know who I'm talking about?"

"That's true." I started laughing to myself because Mr. Thomas was diffidently a character.

"That's why I try to be home by dark, cause freaks aren't the only thing that comes out at night. There's a bunch of strange people around here now."

I could see Keyna walking toward us with her earplugs in singing her little heart out. 'We're beautiful like diamonds in the sky.....' You can't tell her she doesn't sound good and look good with her makeup and fake lashes. Keyna looked older than she really was. I guess having to help raise two younger siblings plus now with a baby of her own will force you to grow up real quick!

"See there, that's what I' talking about right there. Lord, look-a-here, speaking of strange people."

Mr. Thomas shook his head in disappointment.

"Hey Mr. T, hey there Q!" Keyna had her earplugs in so I don't think she realizes how loud she was. On top of that Keyna kinda had a high pitch voice. Mr Thomas had started shutting his eyes tight when she started talking.

"Lord Child, please stop all that yelling and what have you done do to your hair?"

Keyna must get her hair done like every other week and this was her latest style.

"You done gone from crow to chicken."
It was funny watching Keyna roll her eyes but Mr. Thomas was right. She did look a little like a baby chick.

"Girl, I've seen less colors in a rainbow. What you call that right there, Skittles?" Mr. Thomas waves his hand across the in front of her hair. "Taste… the rainbow."

"No Mr. T, I just got my hair done. My girl Taquana she hooked me up."

"Yeah, you're right! Hooked up, snatched up and jacked up."

I could tell by the deep sighs Keyna gave she was getting a little frustrated. "Well my boyfriend likes it, he says it makes me look like a queen."

3

Slightly patting her hair so not to mess it up but Mr. Thomas just busted out laughing. I'm just praying she didn't pay someone to do her hair. I was totally lost for words but Mr. Thomas wasn't.

"Yeah, that's right. Y'all make the perfect couple, Queen Skittles and Goldie Mouth."

Okay, I'm sorry but I had to stop myself from laughing. She did look jacked up and what Mr. Thomas just said was funny as hell.

"Did that boy got a job yet to help you take care of that baby, and why aren't you back in school yet?"

"Well see Mr. T, King is still out studying to be a rapper." Mr. Thomas looks at her totally confused while repeating what she just said, 'studying to be a rapper'. "And I'm about to go to the Cosmetology School so I can get my license to do hair, and we're going to get a place together,"

Mr. Thomas interrupted her. "Hold up Keyna, please tell me how do you *study* to be a rapper?"

"Well, what I mean is that he's at the studio laying down tracks and you know *stuff*."

"Girl, I sure hope you know what you're doing for that baby's sake but you need to go back in school and get a career. Because when I said I wanted you to have a bright and colorful future," Mr. Thomas takes another look at Keyna's hair. "That's not exactly what I had in mind."

We could hear sirens in the distance from the park. It was a sound we were all familiar with so it didn't seem to be a big deal but it was for Mr. Thomas.

"Well- I guess that's my queue to get back to this house." Mr. Thomas had to take his time standing up because of some injury I'm guessing from the war. "Keyna, make sure to tell your momma I said *Hi*."

Keyna sat down on the bench and mumbles under her breath. "Yeah, that's whenever I see her and if she ain't already high"

"Well, you just make sure you take care of yourself and you too Quentin"

Not too many people call me Quentin. But no matter how many times I've told Mr. Thomas my name is Q, he tells me my mommy named me Quentin.

"I wonder why he's always schooling me like he knows everything?"

"You know you can't pay Mr. T no attention Keyna, he's old and doesn't have anybody to talk to."

5

Mr. Thomas always seems to be concerned about us, especially Keyna for some reason. He was always fussing and wanting to know when was she going back to school. Mr. Thomas would tell her to dump that deadbeat, non-rapping, so-called Baby's Daddy. Now Kevin (AKA) King was a pretty well-known local DJ but loves hitting on other girls. It's only a short matter of time before Keyna puts him back in the hospital.

"So Q, what are you doing out here so late? We don't see much of you anymore."

"Well, you know with school and everything I've been busy."

Of course, this wasn't all true. But ever since my dad was in that accident and hurt his leg at work, things had been really tough. Like all the bills have been piling up, and my mom being tired from working two jobs. I don't see things getting any better any time soon.

λ BABY GIRL λ

CHAPTER 2

Graduation was coming up soon and it cost. I was going to have to do something to make this happen. I had tons of stuff to get and things I wanted to do. My Auntie said she was going to look out for me though so that made me feel a little better. Maybe it wasn't that bad! Auntie Andrea was one of my mom's friends from high school so she's kinda like my Godmother. Auntie moved to Atlanta years ago and I've wanted to go there to get away but I never did.

"What's up Q?"

I saw my man Sean walking up with his hand out so I had to give him a dab. Sean was a little smaller than me but we were about the same height. Most of the times he wore glasses but not when we're about to shoot some hoops.

"Nothing much man just waiting on you." I snatch the ball from Sean and started bouncing and showing off some of my LeBron's moves.

"You know we got school tomorrow so let's do this."

"Hi, Keyna." Sean waved his hands in front of Keyna's face to get her attention. She had already put her earplugs back in and was in her own world again.

"Hey, Sean." Keyna pulls one of her earplugs out. "Have you seen Tiffany?"

"Yeah, I saw her earlier with Breanna and Tracey."

I could see Keyna rolling her eyes. I knew she couldn't stand Breanna ever since they almost got into a fight over some guy a few years back.

"So we going to do this are what?" I had already walked off; I wanted to get some shots in before it got too late.

"Oh, I see you're in a hurry to get whooped again."

"Again?" Was this dude out of his mind? "You can't do *nothing* with this!"

Sean was an *ok* player but not good enough to make the cut for the team. But me! I was like *Magic* on the court, but when my grades started slipping my dad made me stop playing.
I admit I was furious at first because that's what everyone knew me for. Plus not to mention being popular at school and especially with the girls. So this last year I was determined to stay focus and get my grades back up, and

with some help of my friend Sean and lots of late night pizzas and curly cheese fires from Tackie's Pizza, I was pretty proud of myself.

"Hey, Tiffany!"

I could hear Keyna from across the park. I glance and saw Tiffany walking toward the park with her backpack on one arm while holding a can of soda. Tiffany has been in love with me since we were two years old. Okay, maybe she's not in love with me but it could happen any day now.

"So Q, have you decided when you want to ride up to the campus to check it out?"

Sean had asked me this *four* times. I really wanted to go like last month but I didn't have my half to give Sean. It's just that right now my money wasn't right.

"Yeah, I'll know something this weekend, and maybe we can stay at my cousin's house and she can show us around the area a little."

"Okay, but let me know something soon cause I just got me some new Jordans and I can't wait to sport them out."

Huh, new Jordans. I remember when I could get just about every one as soon as they hit the shelves. I wouldn't dare show Sean that it bothered me now. "For real man? Well, we're going but I don't think *any* sneakers are going to help you now." I made my way to the hoop with another incredible Q shot. "See that's what's up!"

I was so hype cause I was back on the court with my best friend. If I was going to miss anything, it would be this and without a doubt Tiffany. Ever since middle school, I had a crush on Tiffany. Mostly she stayed to herself and wasn't thinking about boys. But right now, her mind is on Jemar C. Smith. I guess the C stood for conceited, cause he was definitely that. Mr. Jemar is super arrogant and I personally think he's gay. But check this out as I went in for my next shot.

"What?" Sean stood in amaze while the ball circled the rim a few times before dropping in.

"My game is off man." He stood there and shook his head in disbelief.

"Sean, you never had a game."

This wasn't totally true but we haven't had time to play much lately and Sean had missed just about every shot. Sean checked his watch. "Okay, last play man."

Sean volunteers at the Boys Club every Tuesday and Thursday evening. I, on the other hand wanted to volunteer, but I just don't like those kids. They were bad as hell, and I know it would only be a matter of time before I sent one of them home crying.

"Why don't you go and talk to your girl Tiffany?"

Sean took his shot and another one finally went in.

"What for man, she doesn't like me like that. Besides, once we get to Georgia Tech I'll be meeting females left and right."

"That's true." Sean was still bouncing the ball as he started walking off.

"Well, don't forget to give me a call tomorrow."

I heard what Sean was saying but I was thinking about what he said before. Should I go over there and try to talk to her. Hell, why not? I could see Keyna and Tiffany sitting on the park bench. Keyna head was moving from side to side with every word that came out her mouth. The poor girl couldn't get a word in once Keyna got going. Tiffany had no other choice but to listen. 'For Real' and 'Girl Stop' was all you would hear Tiffany say occasionally.

"Hey there girls, and how are you beautiful ladies doing?" A big smile came across Tiffany's face as she said Hi. "So Tiff, what you've been up to cause I haven't seen you lately?"

Tiffany gave a slight sigh. "Just exhausted, I just came from the library and still have a project to turn in by Friday. I'll just be so glad when finals are over."

With that being said, Keyna eyes went back to focus on Tiffany. "Sooo, do this mean you're not going to the party Saturday?"

Tiffany stared at her confused. "What party?"

Keyna looked as if she couldn't believe Tiffany had just said that. Keyna had told me they didn't get to hang out like they use to so Keyna was looking forward to this party. "The one at Rakim's, for his cousin's Getting-Out Party!"

"But I thought that party was last Friday?"

Keyna just shook her head. "No girl, that was a cookout for his *other* cousin."

Okay, so this is about to get good. Cause I knew nothing about any of this.

"See, Ray Ray was the one who got locked up for those carjackings when they busted that strip shop down on 24th and Lee."

Once again, there Keyna goes moving that head side to side. "But Stash was locked up a few years for those robberies up on Madison and 3rd. Girl where you been?"

"Well, obviously *not* on Lee or Madison." Tiffany stood up and grabbed her backpack. "Listen, I'm sure I'll make it to the next one, Rakim's got plenty of cousins so there'll be another party soon. But right now I've got to go home and start on my work."

"I can walk you home Tiff."

Tiffany and I lived on the same street but it wasn't often we got to walk together anymore. I wanted to remember whatever time we could spend together. Who knows, this year just may be our last.

λ ANOTHER WORLD λ
CHAPTER 3

By the time I got to the park the next day, Sean was already there with his ball practicing some shots.

"It's about time you got here." He stopped just long enough to give me one of his disappointed stares, then went in and made another shot.

"I texted you over an hour ago." This time he stops while waiting for an answer.

"I'm sorry man but I had something I had to do."

Sean looks at me like you was totally confused. "And what's that important I had to wait for you this long? It's almost dark."

I tried to come up with a good excuse. "Yeah, I know but I had to pick my brother up from band practice, then run and take my sister over to the library cause my mom had to work late again. So you know I had to, you know take her and everything. Besides, I'm here now!"

Sean looked at me like he didn't really believe me. Then

that silly smile of his came across his face.

"Yeah ok man." Sean tossed me the ball so I could make the next play. "So, I got my letter from Georgia Tech today. Did you check to see if yours came?"
I had the ball in my hand and was focusing on my shot. It was something about playing basketball that made things seem not so bad. I was great on the court and should have tried out again for the team. But I was here now at the park with my best friend.

"No, not yet, but I'm going to check again as soon as I get home." I shot and it's in.

"Well, what about the financial application? Did you do *that* yet?" Sean stood there waiting for me to answer. I stop and closed his eyes as tight as possible because it had completely slipped my mind.

"Oh man, I didn't get a chance to finish it."

I could tell by Sean's reaction that he wasn't buying it. "Q! I told you, you need to get it done to see if it's been approved or not. What are you waiting on?"

Really, I wasn't sure what I was waiting for. But with so much going on I honestly didn't remember. "Yeah I know, but I promise I'll get it done in time." I tried to reassure him that I would get it done. "You know me?"

Sean was still staring at me with that serious look on his face. "Yeah, that's what I'm afraid of. You're always procrastinating on stuff." Then he snatched the ball away from me.

I could see Tiffany as she was walking towards us. I don't know what she sees in Jemar. Word around school is that he's seeing some other girl. I don't know if it's true but if he does *anything* to hurt this girl, you'll be reading about him in his obituary.

"Hi Q."

For a moment I couldn't speak being caught up in the thought on beating her boyfriend down with this baseball bat. "Hey Girl."

She kept looking at me like she wanted to say something but then turned to Sean. "Hey Sean, I'm glad to see you. I need a big favor."

Sean looked a little surprised. "Sure, what's up?"

Tiffany was wringing her hands as if she was a little nervous. "I wanted to ask, do you think you can help me study for my biology finals?"

How could anybody say no to that pretty face and sweet voice?

"Sure, that's no problem."

Sean was really smart but I think I'm pretty smart too so I had to ask. "Heyyy Tiff-a-ny. Now, why didn't you ask me to help you with your bio'logia? And maybe afterward we could go out to dinner, like Burger King or something."

I could tell Tiffany was trying not to laugh too hard so she turned back to Sean. "So…. Anyway, what about tomorrow when you get out from school?"

I knew I couldn't help her with biology. I almost failed it myself last year and this year wasn't looking too good either. But I love messing with Tiffany and making her laugh.

"Hello….." I spoke a little loudly so that I could get her attention.

Tiffany looks at me still trying not to laugh. "Quentin, first of all it's not bio'logia and if I could remember correctly, you had to get help yourself. And second, you don't take a girl out to Burger King for dinner and you don't have your own a car."

I stared at her as if I was hurt but in all honesty, everything she said was true. I was only allowed to drive my mom's car to help her out and go to work. "See there, that what's wrong with you girls now! All because a brother don't have a car. But for you girl, Red Lobster it is!" I throw a wink at her and she had to laugh. Sean just stood there and shook his head.

"So mean to tell me Q, that you got money for Red Lobster?"

I turned and looked at Sean in disbelief. "Of course I have money for Red Lobster."

"Well good, then maybe you can give me back that twenty I loaned you last week?"

Sean and Tiffany started laughing and I had to too because it was pretty funny. I'm just glad he forgot about that 10 I owed him from the week before. "Oh, so you got jokes now, huh Kevin Hart?" I played it off like it was a joke, but the truth was that I had the money. I just couldn't spend it, well at least not now.

"So I'll see you tomorrow?" Tiffany asked Sean but had already started walking away before Sean could answer.

But me, being me had to yell out something to her, as always. "Yeah, and I'll come by too tomorrow! Red Lobster okay. I got you girl!" I watched her as she just shook her head but knew she was laughing inside. "And you can have anything you want!"

She was halfway down the block but I knew she heard me and I left a smile on her face.

"Man I love that girl." Still watching Tiffany as she took a quick glance before crossing the street.

Sean just stood there laughing. "Q, you know she got a boyfriend."

A serious frown came across my face. "That skinny neck, non-playing, Dez Bryant wannabe? Man Please, my grandmamma got better game than he does." I hated Jemar and have thought of plenty of ways to get rid of his punk ass.

Sean raised his eyebrows as if you knew what I was thinking. "Well, you know that wannabe just got accepted to UNC with a four year football scholarship right?"

I knew that! Hell, everyone in school knew that!

"Yeah, he's alright at football, but that brother doesn't have half the skills I process on the court." I reminded Sean as I snatched the basketball away from him.

"Q, you must have forgotten I whipped up on you *just* last week."

Sean was a pretty good ballplayer for his height but there was no way I was going to let him get this one.

"Boy, I've been waiting on you all day." I started bouncing the ball to get my flow. "I'm about to whip you like your grandma did last night when you came home late." I did my famous Q turn and swooped pass Sean. With the ball in my hand, took my aim, it's in the air and it's GOOD!

λ BROKEN PROMISES λ

CHAPTER 4

Jemar was a very popular guy and a lot of girls around here liked him. He fit the perfect profile of an NFL player. He was about 5'11 and the girls thought he was good looking. Me personally, I didn't see where he was all that! But the dude could dress; he always worn the latest style plus he had a car.

"Hey, Tiffany."

Tiffany started smiling as soon as she heard Jemar's voice.

"Let me holla at you a second." Jemar walked over and kissed her on the forehead.

I could see why Tiffany fell for him but couldn't see him being right for her. The first time something starts to go down that brother is going to run. Tiffany needs a *real* man like me, someone who's going to protect her. Everyone knows Jemar can't fight; he's a pretty boy with a pretty game. He would never make it out here in The Aiken and I'll bet all my Uncle Rob's crack on that.

"Hey Baby, how are things going?" Tiffany asked

but her smile went away when she noticed the serious look on his face. "Is everything okay?" She was hoping it was but lately most of his discussions were about them having sex or not. Tiffany wasn't ready to talk about it, at least not now or at least not here.

"Yeah Baby, everything is cool, I was just wondering if you were coming by my place after school?"

Even though no one was close enough to hear what they were talking about Tiffany was still uncomfortable talking about it. "Jemar, you know we got finals coming up and I have,"

"Listen, I just need to know what's up with you?" He wasn't waiting for another one of her excuses. "You either want to be with me or not Tiffany?"

Tiffany knew by the tone of his voice that he was getting agitated. She was falling for this guy and hated the thought of losing him to someone else. "Okay, I can stop by for a little while."

"Good, I see you later then."

Tiffany watched Jemar as he walked down the hallway yelling at some guys he sometimes hung out with. *'What am I going to do?'* For the first time in years, she was confused. Tiffany was the smart one, the one who had it all together when it came to knowing what she wanted in life.

What if this will be a huge mistake? What if the rumors are true about him talking to other girls? Jemar was her first real boyfriend but he has had plenty other girlfriends. Yet he made her feel like she had been the only one he ever loved and she didn't want to lose that.

Θ

All I know is the way that I feel,
And all I know is that these feelings are real.
But just the thought of him or if I hear his name,
What will I do if he doesn't feel the same?
Right now I don't know what to do,
Can you explain IT because I need to hear from you.
Late at night when I feel all alone,
In a world that makes you feel so cold.
Don't want to lose his love and let him down
But I get so weak whenever he's around
And I cannot hide the things I feel inside
So please tell me IT or is it all just a lie?

Tiffany couldn't let her mother see her like this. Ms. Alston would know immediately that something was bothering her. Ms. Alston was very protective of Tiffany but I couldn't really blame her. Tiffany would have to lie if her mother asked where she'd been. And of course, she's going to ask!

"Hey Sweetie, how was school today?" Ms. Alston was stooping down going through the pots in one of the kitchen cabinets. "That stewed chicken will be done soon and I'll put on some rice before I leave for choir practice."

There was always sometime going on at Holy Trinity Baptist Church and Ms. Alston was usually a part of it. She's always talking about how some people in the church don't help to do anything. But the same people always have something negative to say about everything.

"It was good Momma." Tiffany would normally head straight to the kitchen to help out but she just wanted to get to her room. "Still have a lot of work to do, so I'll get something later."

Tiffany room was small but she loved it. For her 12th birthday, her mom let Mr. Anderson painted it for her. She chose her favorite color blue and decorated it with lots of pillows and stuffed animals she collected over the years. Keyna spent most of her time there because there were so many siblings, nieces, and nephews over at her place. Keyna would tell her how lucky she was to have her own room but Tiffany didn't feel safe there anymore. *IT* had too many secrets and she kept them in her diary. *IT* let her talk about things she could not tell anyone, not even her best friend. *IT* was easier that way.

Θ

No one can ever know what's really on my mind
The things that I truly desire
Know the pain that I feel and things that I'm so afraid of
Only IT can know and IT would never tell
IT would ever reveal my nightmares
The bad dreams have finally gone away
Because IT kept my safe

You know I always try my best to do the right things. I study
very hard and help people whenever I can. I love my family
and grateful for all my friends and going to miss everyone
when I leave here. Jemar and I will be going off to different
colleges and I don't know what's going to happen between
us. I'm afraid that when he leaves, our relationship is going
to be over. I love him so much! I don't want to let him go,
but if I don't sleep with him then he'll just be with
someone else. I'm asking IT to help me. So please tell
me if IT's right. Please tell me this!

Ms. Aston had already left by the time Tiffany came out of her room. Tiffany wasn't that hungry until the smell of the stewed chicken hit her. Tiffany was just in the middle of eating when Kenya knocked on the door.

"Girl, I'm just in time." Keyna walked in pushing Lil' Kevin in his Winnie the Pooh stroller. Tiffany went over to pick Lil' Kevin up while Keyna went straight to the kitchen. "I brought the baby by so you could see him."

27

Keyna yelled to Tiffany over the sound of the water from the kitchen sink.

Tiffany started laughing. She was actually glad they had stopped by. "Is that the only reason you came here?"

"Girl please!" Keyna finished washing and drying her hands. "You know I had to come by to get something to eat." Keyna had already grabbed a plate from the kitchen cabinet and was in the pots.

"Lil' Kevin, I can't believe how big you're getting."

Lil' Kevin would soon be 1 year old and Tiffany already had in mind what she wanted to do for his 1st birthday.

"Is he walking on his own yet?" Tiffany was no longer interested in her dinner. She just wanted to see if she could get Lil' Kevin to stand on his own and take a few steps.

"No, he's just pulling everything down or trying to hit everybody with something."

"Well, I guess he takes that after his mother."

"I don't be pulling anything down!" Keyna went and sat down at the kitchen table. "Well, at least not anymore."

"Yeah, but you still be hitting and fighting people Keyna."

Keyna definitely had some anger issues. I once saw her beat up the school bully, bit a teacher *and* got suspended. And that was all in the first grade. "I got to work on that cause my probation officer said I might not make bail the next time."

"I still don't see how you made bail the last time."

Keyna was too busy eating and talking about how good the food was. "See, why can't my mom cook like this?"

"But you know how to cook Keyna. Don't you cook sometimes at the house?"

Keyna stopped eating and looked at Tiffany. "Hell no! I don't cook at that house anymore. The last few times I tried, them kids ate all the food out the pot before it was even finished."

Tiffany started laughing again. "Well, you know my mom cooks around here like she's trying to feed a whole army."

"Yes, and that's why I'm here."

λ DON'T BOTHER ME λ

CHAPTER 5

I couldn't believe it was almost time for graduation. We all had so much stuff going on it was unreal! Auntie Andrea had taken off from work because her father wasn't doing well. I knew she would have helped me out if she could but things happen. It was cool though because I had a plan. Sean didn't have much to worry about. He's been working down at the supermarket for the past two years and they loved him there. His boss is always sliding him a little extra something for school. Plus his grandmother had retired and her husband had deceased. So she had a couple of checks coming in every month. As for Tiffany, her mother never let her go without. Ms. Alston would work five jobs if she had to. She had to have been part Jamaican or something. Either way, Tiffany was straight.

Things at home weren't getting any easier. My mom was always tired from working so I try to do what I can around the house. Dad wasn't home yet; I'm not sure where he spends most of his day anymore. I think he kinda got tired of looking for a job and started back hanging out with his partners. My dad always worked and I know it's killing him not to be able to bring home any money.

31

"You need to make sure those dishes are cleaned before momma gets here." I don't know why I have to keep telling my little sister that. Kimberly was only 10 years old but very smart and knew momma liked to keep everything clean and in place. She was lying on the sofa watching some show on her phone as usual.

"I'm going to do it!" I heard her suck her teeth and mumbled something under her breath. It didn't matter as long as she got it done. I took a quick look around to see if anything else needed to be done.

"So Kim, where's Omar?"

"I don't know." She didn't bother looking up from her phone.

Omar was only a year younger than me but he was much smaller. My brother had some challenges due to being born with Phenylketonuria. Lots of people thought he was much younger. They would treat him more like a little kid which he hated.

"Well, I'm about to jump in the shower before I go to work."

Normally I would check to make sure Omar's okay but he's probably at one of his friend's house. Besides, I didn't want to be late for work but I had something important to do first. "So don't forget about those dishes." Once again she acted like she was ignoring me, but she knew it better get done!

Night time was a whole other story in Aiken Park. I was wishing my cousin would hurry up and get here. I wasn't trying to be out here too long just in case somebody rolled up on me unexpectedly. Even worst, someone sees me and it got back to my dad. EZ was always cool but my dad didn't like that he sold drugs. He lived with us for a little while until my dad out him found drugs and a gun in our room. Then I spotted someone pulling up in a badass red Infinity Q60 with some Volk Rims. I assumed it was EZ cause he stays popping a nice ass ride. Yeah, it was him. I saw he had some dude with him and they were discussing something about a game.

"What's up Lil' Cuz?" EZ opened his door and got out. Man is it just my imagination or did this dude blow up since the last time I saw him. But the brother was sharp! I mean he be shopping at Prada and Saks Fifth Avenue over in New York.

See, that's where I need to be getting my gears from. I hardly see anybody around The Aiken with clothes like that. EZ walked up and gave me a hug. Now, I know I'm not gay but whatever cologne that brother was wearing was *nice*. I got to get me some of that shit! "You man." For real, I was still trying to get over that cologne.

"So how's everything, Aunt Dee and everybody

doing okay?"

I noticed he didn't ask about my dad but I didn't expect him to. I knew EZ was the only son my dad's sister had. My dad did try to help keep him out of trouble but EZ did whatever EZ wanted to. So after he left from where we were staying, he was back on the street and then back in jail. "Yeah, everybody is good, and how about you?"

EZ took a step back and throw his arms open showing off his outfit that was probably more then what I made in 4 months. "Do you have to ask?"

"True." Now thats what I need and then Tiffany would be all over me like.

"Listen EZ." I took a deep breath before I could try and get my words out. "Things are really tight right now and I just need your help."

I also may need his help making my funeral arrangements, cause my dad is going to kill me if he found out I'm out here with him.

"Okay, so what do you need?"

"Well, I'm just going to be honest with you. I was hoping you could hook a brother up and let me make some runs for you."

EZ started snickering and put his hand up to his mouth. I didn't see what in the hell was funny.

"Listen, I'm been trying to work over at BJ's Grocery Store but the pay sucks. My dad still hasn't been able to find another job yet and my mom is holding down two jobs just to make ends meet. It just ain't getting it Cuz."

I could tell EZ knew I was serious. He still had his hand covering his mouth but was nodding his head in agreement. "No doubt Lil' Cuz, I hear you but I don't know."

"Look EZ, we're like behind on bills and the mortgage. If something doesn't happen soon we'll be out on the streets. Besides, things will get caught up before he even knows anything."

"Alright then." EZ pulls his phone out from his pocket. "Give me a minute."

EZ walked off a little and soon heard him talking to someone on the other end. I could see the dude in the car looking around with all guards up. Hell, looked like he was more nerves than me.

"Okay, I think I got a little something to help you out with." EZ put his phone away and headed back towards me.

"That's whats up Lil' Cuz" I could tell he was still a little skeptical. "Just meet me back out here tomorrow night, got it?"

"No problem EZ, I'll see you tomorrow."

EZ gave me another dab and hug. Man! I need to find out where he got that cologne from.

Things were starting to change for the better. I had been so occupied with making runs for EZ; it's been a minute since I was able to meet up with Sean. I needed to talk to him because this Boys Club thing just wasn't going to work out for me.

"Q, you've only been there for like three weeks and you're talking about quitting already?"

I was still bouncing the ball but then stood up straight so that Sean could hear loud and clear what I was about to say.

"Sean, I'm not just quitting. I'm planning on pressing charges on some of those kids." I started bouncing the ball again but still couldn't seem to get a good rhythm.

"Q, they're only like nine and ten years old. Besides, you can't just give up on them like that."

"Well, their parents have already given up on them like that! That's why they send them to the Boys Club. Man Sean, I can't do anything with those bad behind Hood

Pack! You're on your own Homie." I pass the ball to Sean hoping he would have better luck with a shot than me.

"We're supposed to take the boys bowling this weekend so you know those kids going to be looking for you?"

"Yeah, they may be looking but I promise they won't find me!"

Okay, so maybe I did not make myself clear enough to Sean. So let me break it down so he'll understand. We'll just stop playing ball altogether for a minute.

"Listen, I tried okay! But the last time we took those kids bowling, they pasted M&Ms to the back of my brand new jersey. Then they went and crazy glued some of the bowling balls together so now we can't even go back there. Then one kid tried to flush a stack of paper towels down the toilet and we had to stay and clean that mess up. And I still don't know what that smell is but I *can't* get it out my Jordans." By this time I'm starting to get pissed off all over again because I wasn't even finished yet. "And *please* tell me how you're going to steal all the people's toilet tissue, wait until I have to go, and then try to sell it back to me? Man, you must be crazy!"

"Q, you're just saying that, right?"

While Sean was distracted from laughing, I snatched the ball and went in hard for a quick shot but missed. "See that's why my game is so off! See, look at my hand." I held it out to Sean. "My hand is still shaking from outing that fire one of them started in my back seat. Man, that's my momma's car! And where in the hell they get a lighter from?" I started shaking my head because I still couldn't believe what those boys did. On top of that, I couldn't believe how off my shots were. I mean they were *way* off.

"Listen Q, I'm sorry." Yeah, even though Sean was saying he was sorry, he was still laughing. "You have to understand, these are underprivileged kids and they have nowhere else to go. Besides, this is our last year and it would really look good on your transcript. Plus Tiffany is impressed with your commitment to these kids."

I had to take a deep breath but Sean did make some good points. And Tiffany has been much nicer to me lately.

"Alright then, but you can tell The Hood Pack I'm bringing my Taser. And the *first* one that steps out of line, I swear I'm taking them out, I promise you that!"

λ ANYTHING FOR LOVE λ
CHAPTER 6

Bible Study wasn't usually over until after 9 o' clock and even then Ms. Alston wouldn't get home for another hour. Tiffany had told her mother that she was going to the library to study with Brenna just in case her mother got back early. Tiffany had felt horrible about lying but she had to see Jemar. She loved him and she wanted to prove it to him. She just needed to know that he felt the same way too.

Keyna had warned Tiffany about making sure to take some protection. She told Tiffany that King had sworn he had some but of course, that was a total lie. The last thing Tiffany needed was to get pregnant. It wasn't that she didn't want to have a baby for him but just not now. They have their whole lives to spend together and tonight was going to be their night.

"Hey Baby, how are you?"

Jemar was sitting on the sofa with his cousin Antone and one of his friends from school. Tiffany had no idea what to say. There were several beer cans on the coffee table. They were laughing and joking while listening to a music video and playing a game on the PlayStation. She was expecting them to be alone so what in the hell were they doing here?

"I thought you wanted me to come by so we could talk." It was a little hard for Tiffany to get her words out. Maybe she had misunderstood what he had said earlier.

"Yeah, Baby." Jemar stood up and walked over to Tiffany and gave her a slight kiss. "Hey guys, this is my baby Tiffany."

There was something about the way he called her Baby that she loved about him. Tiffany gave out a slight '*Hi*' and then looked at Jemar. "Listen Jemar, I really wanted to talk to you about something."

"Sure, we can go to my room and talk."

He must be out of his black mind! "Um, I think we should talk outside."

Jemar started laughing then walked back over and grabbed his beer off the table. "No, come on let's go to my room for a minute." He went back over and took her hand but Tiffany pulled away. It was not about to go down like that.

"Girl what's the matter with you?" Jemar started getting loud as if to flex his authority. He wasn't about to let some girl disrespect him in front of his boys.

"Well, I need to talk to you."

"And I said we can talk in the room."

Tiffany just stared at Jemar for a second. For some reason, he was acting different. She had never seen Jemar like this before. Was it the beer or the weed? It was hard to tell but was smelt before you hit the front porch. "I'll talk to you later."

"No, I don't think so Tiffany."

What did he just say? He don't think so? What is going on with him? "Jemar, I don't want to go in no bedroom with you."

Jemar had already started walking away. He sat down and start looking back at the video before Tiffany could finish. "You can go."

Jemar took another drink of beer and just stared at the TV as if she wasn't even there. He had just told her she could go but she couldn't move. Was he putting me out because I wouldn't have sex with him while his friends were in the next room? Did he think I was some T.H.O.T.? This couldn't be real, it was just another one of her dreams. That's it, it's just another bad dream.

Finally, I was off work and couldn't wait to get home. I was wondering what Mon had cooked or picked up for dinner tonight. Either way, she always had something good to eat. I speeded up a little because a brother was hungry. But then I saw Tiffany sitting on the swing in the park by herself. 'What in the hell is she doing out here this late?' The bus stop was just across the street. Maybe she was waiting for Ms. Alston to come home. I'll just go over and check to make sure everything's okay.

"Hey Tiff, what are you doing?"

Tiffany was still in a daze and didn't even see when I pulled up. I saw as I got closer that she seemed very upset. "Oh, hey Q."

"Is everything okay?"

I parked the car and got out to walk over to her. I knew the bus would be coming soon but Ms. Alston wouldn't want her out here by herself. "Tiffany, are you alright?"

Tiffany shook her head before bursting into tears. I hurried to turn the car off and got out the car to go over to hug her. I had never seen her cry before and I just needed to know what to do to make her feel better.

"Tiffany, what's wrong, what happened?"

Tiffany couldn't speak so I just let her cry until she was ready to talk. "Jemar just broke up with me."

You have got to be kidding me! Did she just say what I thought she said? "Y'all broke up?"

Tiffany nodded her head as she wipes tears away from her eyes.

"Well, what happened?" Because I need to know, I need details.

"He got upset with me because I wouldn't sleep with him so he told me to leave."

"For real!" I couldn't believe this. So that meant they didn't have sex that night they went to prom? Thank you Lord, there is a God! "Listen Tiff, that brother doesn't deserve the time of day from you. He's just another part-time player wishing he was a pimp. You are so smart and beautiful, plus you're always nice to people and you are so beautiful. And you are so talented and gifted, plus you are so beautiful."

Tiffany couldn't help but laugh even though she was hurting inside. "But I thought he really loved me. I thought we were meant to be together and I wanted to spend the rest of our lives together."

Okay, so what does a brother say after hearing something like that? "Listen, Tiffany...." I had to think of something to say, even though I really just wanted to run Jemar's head through a center block. 'Okay Q, stay focus'. "We have to realize that things don't always turn out the way we plan." Hum, I should know from my own personal experiences. "But that doesn't mean things won't get better. You just have to keep the faith and trust in God, and trust in yourself."

"I'm just so tired of all the games and disappointments Q. I really think he's seeing someone else."

She thinks but I know! But this was neither the time nor the place, she was hurting and that was hurting me. Tiffany closed her eyes and took a deep sight. Even with the tears, she was still amazing.

"Well if he is then he's just crazy. Cause there's no way I would ever let someone like you go."

Another smile came across her face which made me felt better. The lights of the midtown bus were approaching. That was normally the bus Ms. Alston took home. Tiffany tried to dry her face before the bus came to its stop. She didn't want her mother to see that she had been crying. Obviously, this Jemar has no idea that I knew people and they can make it as if he ever even existed.

λ REAC TACK λ
CHAPTER 7

Sean spent time with Tiffany studying for her finals in biology. She already had a 4.0 GPA and took advanced courses in just about every class. She was already awarded some scholarships and several colleges had written her. I knew Tiffany was determined to get as less grants as possible. The last thing she wanted was to have her mother worrying about how college was going to get paid.

"I think you got this Tiff." Sean reassured her as she glanced across her notebook.

"Yeah, I hope so."

Sean was an excellent tutor. Anyone who could help me up my grades had to be.

"Listen, you're going to do great, you always do."

When Sean saw her smile, he could tell she was feeling better about the whole thing.

"Thanks again for your help, you are so good at this

stuff."

"Oh, I see the student has become the master." Sean proclaimed in his Chinese voice.

"Well, if you need help with anything just let me know."

Sean remembers that he still had things to do for the Boys Club. "What about making up some permission slips for our bowling night?"

"Sure, I can do that."

"Great." Sean looked through his backpack and found a flyer. "This has all the information on it and if you can have them by the weekend that would be great."

"No problem Sean." Tiffany took the flyer and looked over it. She was impressed that he was still doing so much, especially with finals so close. "I don't understand how you find the time to do all this stuff. I hardly have enough time to go to my classes and get my homework done."

Sean thought about it for a moment. He didn't really think about it because some things just came easily to him.

"Well, my classes are only half a day and I work about 20 hours a week." Sean pauses to remember if he was forgetting anything. "And the Boys Club is only on Tuesdays and Thursdays. So I'm straight."

"Yeah, but I still don't see how you do it. But I really admire you for helping out those kids like that."

Ms. Alston had just come in the door and Tiffany could tell right away that it had been another long day for her.

"Lord... I will be so glad when they hire some more people at that place. They really try to kill the few that's there." After taking a sigh of relief, Ms. Alston sat her purse on the entry table and headed straight to the sofa and sat down.

"You mean to tell me they still haven't hired more people yet?"

Tiffany knew her mom had been saying this for weeks. Her mom had given up her manager position after eight years because it was too stressful. This was the time of the year the hotel was starting to get busy.

"Yeah, but I'm thankful that I at least have a job." Ms. Alston had already slipped into her house shoes. She always kept them by the sofa so she could put her feet up and rest them on the coffee table. "Well, how is everything going with you Sean?"

"I'm doing great Ms. Alston, it sounds like you had

47

a pretty rough day."

"I'm okay Sweetie. My feet just hurt some after being on them all day. Then walking to and from that bus stop doesn't help any."

Ms. Alston was not a small woman, and the only time you would see her was usually at the bus stop. I don't believe it was because she couldn't afford a car, I think she just never bothered to learn how to drive. "Look like the more I walked the further the house moved away."

Sean and Tiffany started snickering but Ms. Alston was serious and kept a straight face. "I'm thinking about getting one of those electric scooters to ride back and forth there."

Sean was still snickering but Tiffany was hoping her mom was just kidding. She could only imagine her mother on one and get teased about it. The kids around there could be very cruel and some adults were even crueler.

"Momma, please don't do that." Tiffany was definitely serious.

"Oh, don't worry baby. I'll make sure I get a two-seater so you can ride too."

Sean was trying his best to stop laughing while Tiffany stared at her mother in shock. "That's right Ms. Alston, I heard about those. They got the one now with the two seats side by side and an alarm so nobody can just ride off in it."

Tiffany thought they both had lost their minds. She knew she had to intervene in this discussion. "Those things only go like 10 MPH so how do you think someone could just ride off with one?"

Sean and Ms. Alston had this conversation, so at this time Tiffany didn't even exist. "Plus they come with a horn, Ms. Alston."

"For real?" Ms. Alston was now on the sofa facing Sean.

"Yeah, that way you can blow at the people in your way before you run them over."

"Man, that's a good idea!"

Tiffany could see this conversation had taken a turn for the worst. "Isn't it time for you to leave?" Tiffany said it more as a command than a question.

"No, not really." Sean knew he had to go but it was always fun joking around with Ms. Alston. Tiffany tried to keep a straight face because she knew they were only kidding her.

"Bye, Sean!" Tiffany got up to give him the hint that it was time for him to go. Sean grabbed his backpack and walked over to Ms. Alston.

"Bye, Ms. Alston." Sean bent over and gave Ms. Alston a kiss on her cheek.

"Good Bye Sweetie, and please tell your Grandma that I said *Hello*."

"I sure will Ms. Alston." Sean headed for the door where Tiffany was already waiting. "Hey Ms. Alston, can you let Tiffany pick me up when you get your scooter so we can take a ride downtown?"

"Sure!" Ms. Alston said without any hesitation.

"Get out Sean!"

λ HUSTLING FOR A DOLLAR λ

CHAPTER 8

I was feeling so much better being able to help out with some of the bills. I told them that I had picked up some extra hours at work. Of course, I couldn't let my parents know what I was doing. But it kept us from being in the dark and without water. EZ had really hooked me up! I could see how it would be so simple to get caught up in. But I had other plans and it didn't involve me being locked up in some prison. That if I even made it to prison. Yeah, I'm definitely sure my dad will kill me first.

"Hey, there Q." EZ was laughing as he pulled up to the park. "So, what's up Lil' Cuz?"

I jumped in and he looked over at me with a smile that reminded me of the Joker. Hell, I guess I would be smiling too if I had the money he had. "Nothing much EZ." I had no idea where we were going and in this game its best not to ask too many questions.

"Good, good. So all your people doing okay?"

"Yeah, everybody is good man." I was nervous as hell but this was not the time. I had things to do and money to make. Besides, EZ has been doing this for a long time so I have nothing to worry about? Right? "Yeah, hmm." I was trying to start up a conversation but what do we have in common to talk about anymore? "Did I tell you I'm going to college this fall?"

"No... For real man!" EZ glanced over at me and the Joker's smile was gone quick! "Well, that's great Lil' Cuz. Hey, but don't worry, I'm not going to let nothing happen to you."

I was so glad he could read my mind. I know he said we weren't going far but this seemed like a long ass ride. I just wanted to hurry and get this over with. "Listen, if I could get all the stuff for college, I won't have to ask my mom for nothing. You know what I mean, right?"

"Yeah, no doubt, I understand Lil' Cuz."

I don't know much about this side of town but heard it was pretty rough. Hell, I lived in the hood but this was the hood-hood. It was getting late and little kids were running around like it was still day. *And what is that smell?* It smelled like the whole neighborhood was sitting inside a big ass huffy trash bag. And was that Satan I just saw standing on the corner?

"You know Lil' Cuz, everything I got, I got it on

my own."

I was caught up in the scenery so I wasn't really listening. EZ was talking about how hard his past life was. But from where I was sitting, Cuz was doing pretty good now. "See man, I want to be riding around in a car like this. And buying expensive shit that most people around here ain't even heard of."

EZ's laughter made me think back on the time we stole his mom's boyfriend car. That guy was so mad at us by the time we got back. He took off while cursing us out, but we never had to worry about seeing him again.

"Hold up Lil' Cuz. I know you want to get it and there's mad paper to be made out here." EZ pulled a huge roll of bills from underneath his seat. *'What the fxxx!'* How in the hell did he get an ATM up under there? "I'm telling you, I can hook you up with anything you need. Just look at me!"

I'm sorry, but I couldn't look because the roll of dollars had me hypnotized. I've never held that much money before in my life; it had to be about 3 or 4 grands.

"Here's an early graduation present. I told you I'd look out for you." EZ was saying something or maybe singing freestyle like he did back in the day. But I wasn't hearing *anything*! So excuse me while I count this money.

Θ

"I've been down for so long,
everything I did it seemed so wrong.
Didn't stay in school just not my style,
too much time not worth my while.
I got to get mine and I can't wait,
you better get yours for it's too late.
Take my advice cause this is true,
going to tell you how and what to do.
So if you wanna be, anything like me.
Stop wasting your time, cause right here you'll find.
I got money, so much money.
Plenty for the honeys and I know
that you want to be like me."

Hold up! EZ just mentioned two of my favorite things, 'Money and Honeys'. Okay, now he had my undivided attention.

"I got dollars and, it makes you wanna holler.
I spend it by the hours and I know
that you want to be like me.

No one gave me a chance to show,
all of the things that I did know.
They treated me bad all the time,
I thought I was going to lose my mind.

54

I realized I was on my own,
when my Mother left me all alone.
But now I got things I never had,
diamond rings and money by the bags.
So if you wanna be, anything like me.
Stop wasting your time, cause right here you'll find.
I got money, so much money.
Plenty for the honeys and I know
that you want to be like me."

Man, my cousin had it all and started showing me stuff with names I couldn't even pronounce.

"Okay, so when I pull up to here, I just need you to look out for anything that doesn't look right. I always keep a piece in here just in case." EZ reached over by my leg to open the glove compartment. A Glock 36 pistol was staring right at me.

Now, I had seen guns before but this dude is talking about me grabbing this if I need it. He must not know me because this car is still running. I'm going to beep the horn one time as a signal, *'To get the hell out'*, and then I'm gone.

"Man EZ, I never shot at anybody before." This shit was becoming too real too fast for me.

"Nothing is going to happen; it's just there for an emergency."

Emergency! We have a first aid kit and a flashlight for emergencies at my house, not no gun. And this one looked like he had an attitude. As if he'll accidentally go off just because he's having a bad day.

"Okay, Cuz." I mean, what else could I have said? I was in this now and I was running too close to turn back now. But you can best believe a brother will be putting down some serious praying. *'Lord, can you please help a brother out!'*

λ WATCH YOURSELF λ

CHAPTER 9

People here are real lucky to get out of this place. For the most part, it was either when you got locked up or when you died. Sometimes I thought the ones who died was luckier. I've seen what can happen to some of the guys who got locked up. They came out of prison with nowhere to go so they felt they're better off back in prison. And if getting a job without a rap sheet wasn't hard enough. Then you can only imagine how it is with one.

"I'm going to kill him when I see him again." Keyna could be heard all the way on the other side of the park. "He can say whatever he wants but I'm not playing with his punk ass." Keyna was on the phone talking to one of her sisters and she was mad as hell. "I don't care about none of that! I'm out here doing the best I can."

Keyna had been crying and was still upset so whatever her sister was trying on Keyna, she wasn't hearing it. "I go to work every day to take care of me and my son. Oh, but this shit here ain't going to happen again."

Tiffany had rushed over to the park because Keyna had asked to meet her there.

"Girl, I'm going to have to call you back." Keyna hung up with her sister and went to meet Tiffany. "Hey, Tiffany."

"Is everything okay, what's going on?"

Keyna shook her head and then started crying again. "I can't believe this." Keyna blurted out and sat down on the bench. Tiffany sat beside her and started rubbing her shoulder to console her.

"Keyna, what's wrong, are you alright?"

Keyna was still shaken up and was trying to calm herself down. "I can't believe it Tiff, King took all the money."

Tiffany wasn't exactly clear on what Keyna was talking about. "What, what money?"

"The money I had to pick up some food." Tiffany has never seen Keyna this upset before. "Girl, that punk ass negro took the money so he can go hang out with his friends."

Tiffany was just as confused as to how King could do something so stupid! "Why would he even do that? He knows you have to get food for you and the baby."

"I mean after everything I've done for him. I let him stay over at my place when he couldn't get a ride home.

I'm giving his sorry ass money so he won't be wearing the same clothes over and over. I'm taking care of his child while he's at some studio all night. And I ain't seen one record deal yet!"

OMG, Keyna was mad as hell. Everyone knew that Keyna was crazy about King, but now she was just crazy. "Then he turns around and steals from me? Girl, he done lost his mind for real." Poor Tiffany wanted to get a word in, but Keyna was nowhere near to being finish yet. "And the times I thought he was out there looking for a job, *please*. His sister told me he be right at Ray Ray's house getting high." Yeah, it's in full effect now because there she goes with those hands with every word that comes out of Keyna's mouth. "And on top of that, he has the nerve to cuss me out when I asked him what happened to the money."

Keyna finally paused but Tiffany didn't know if that was a question or a statement.

"But he should know that I ain't the one." Okay, so I guess it was a statement then. "I promise I'm going to slice up every stitch of clothes he owns. Rather he's in it or not."

Tiffany finally had a chance to break in and say something. "Man Keyna, I can't believe he took the money like that. I know how bad you must feel."

Keyna looked over at Tiffany and her voice was now calm. "No you don't Tiff, you got it made. You have a mother who loves and cares about you. My mother doesn't care anything about me or my sister. The only thing she cares about is where she's getting more crack from. I mean, do you have any idea what it's like to have a mother who's strung out on drugs?"

Tiffany couldn't look Keyna in the eyes because she couldn't even begin to imagine that.

"Ever since I was little I hated going to school! The only clothes we had were clothes other people gave us, and my mother wouldn't even take the time to wash those. We got teased just about every single day! Tiffany, there were times we didn't have food or lights. So that's why when I met King I thought things would be different. I don't want my son to go through what I went through. And I don't want him growing up without his father like I did."

Tiffany wasn't quite sure how to respond. She always knew that Keyna had it rough coming up but never knew she felt that way. Now she understood why Keyna acted so tough and fearless. I guess we all have things we hold inside. But sooner or later, it has to come out and it not always in a good way. "Well, is there anything I can do to help?"

Keyna shook her head. "No, I guess I just needed someone to talk to that's all."

"Well listen, I've got $40 at the house you can have so you can get some food for you and the baby."

"Tiffany, you know I can't take any money from you. You're trying to get things together before leaving for college."

"Girl, I'll be fine. Besides, I wouldn't be able to sleep knowing my godson don't have anything to eat. You know that boy's a big eater."

Tiffany finally got a small laugh from her. Keyna didn't want to take the money but Tiffany insisted.

"So where is King now?"

"Oh, yeah girl. He's at the hospital."

"The hospital!" Tiffany couldn't believe Keyna hadn't mentioned that. "Are you serious Keyna?"

Keyna nodded her head.

"Why is King at the hospital?"

"Well, what happened was. I was talking to him right, and he started getting loud with me. And I was holding a glass bottle and it just slipped out my hand, a couple of times. So his arms and shoulders and stuff got a little cut up, and I think his head got busted up a little."

Keyna shook her head again. "But… It didn't look too good girl."

"Keyna, are you serious?" Tiffany had to ask again because she couldn't believe what she was hearing.

"Yeah, but I did call someone to come get him and everything." Keyna paused to make sure she wasn't forgetting anything. "Hum, I don't know what happened to him after that cause I left."

I can't believe this girl! She done killed Kevin and Tiffany is going to be convicted for concealing information after the fact. I can't have my future baby's momma locked up. Sure, Keyna would do okay in prison but my poor Tiffany wouldn't last a day.

λ NIGHTMARES λ

CHAPTER 10

My phone has been going off nonstop these last few weeks. I was starting to make money hand over fist and everything was looking good. Before you know it, I'll be able to get me a nice ride before heading to college. Maybe even get a chance to take Tiffany out and buy her some things that Mr. Jemar couldn't get her. Of course, I've been putting most of the money away so my parents wouldn't be too suspicious. They have been asking me how was I able to help out with the bills, but told them my boss had me working a lot of over time. This would also account for all the extra time I've been spending away from home. Man, I got another call but this time it was my boy, Sean.

"Hey, Sean what's up?"

"Man, I've been trying to reach you all day!"

I did see when he was trying but I was on business calls. "Yeah, I know man but I was just busy all day."

"Well listen, were you still planning on coming out to the Boys Club?"

Seriously I had already forgotten about that but I knew Tiffany was impressed about Sean being involved with helping those kids. So 'Hell Yeah' I was going. "Sure, I'll be there."

I was hoping that Tiffany would be available to talk when I call. She and Jemar weren't on good term so we've been talking about a lot of things. I had noticed she seems to a little unhappy but not exactly sure why. Maybe it's because she's afraid of leaving her mom or her and Jemar breakup. Well, whatever it is, I'm determined to find out because I can't have my princess unhappy like this.

"Hello."

Great, she picked up. "Hey Tiffany, how's everything going girl?"

"Everything is still good and how are you?"

I was feeling great! I had just eaten some of my mom's fried chicken with some collard greens. I had the room all to myself so I was just relaxing while Omar was out with some of his friends. "I'm doing good too and just wondering if you want to hang out a little later?"

"Well, I'm not sure yet."

"Why, do you already have other plans?" Because if she was just going to b sitting around doing nothing, I was about to change that!

"No, not really."

"Okay Tiffany, please talk to me. I need you to tell me what's really going on. Is it Jemar?"

"No, he's the last person on my mind right now." Now that's what I really wanted to hear.

"So tell me what it is then?"

"Well..." Tiffany pauses for a moment. "It's really crazy and I don't even know how to explain it."

"If you tell me what it is maybe I can help." I couldn't hear anything and almost thought she was no longer there, but then she spoke.

"I've been having these crazy nightmares that seem so real."

Tiffany pauses again. I guess she was waiting for a response but I didn't know what to say.

"What kind of nightmares?" This was the kind of stuff my grandmother was good at interpreting. The only nightmares I had was when I was little when I thought the Boogie Man was hiding under my bed. But my dad reassured me that the Boogie Man never came to the hood because he was afraid he would get robbed.

"It's like when I'm asleep someone is there standing over me and when I try to get up I can't even move."

Maybe it was something she ate because I heard that gave people nightmares but I couldn't say that, it sound too stupid. "So have you told your mom about them?"

"No, I don't want to worry her, besides I don't want to get her started with her getting her oil and laying her hand praying for me."

Yeah, she was right about that! I remembered the last time Ms. Alston heard I was acting up in school and decided to pray for me. She had some *holy* oil and laid her hand on me and started praying. I had enough oil on my forehead to fry a whole pan of chicken.

"I couldn't see the person's face but I know it was a man. A tall slender man with glasses and I could smell Old Spice Shaving Cologne."

Old Spice! Not only was this fool bothering my boo, but he had no taste at all. "So Tiffany, do you think with all the changes that have been going on and you're leaving home has anything to do with it?"

"Yes, I thought about that too but I've been having these dreams for a while. I just haven't told anyone about them."

Damn, so she means that I'm the only person she'd told this to. I didn't know what to think but I felt privileged that she shared this with me. So now I have to find a way to help her cause the last thing I would want to do is disappoint her. "Tiffany, I hate to even say this." I had to stop and think because I didn't want to upset her any more than she was already. "But can you remember anything, maybe something that might have happened in the past?"

Wow, I don't even know where that came from. But I remembered me and EZ would sneak out of bed at night because we couldn't sleep. We would overhear our moms and their friend talk about everything, and I do mean *everything*. I heard their friend saying how her cousin would come into her room and molest her. He had told her that he would kill her if she ever told anyone, so she didn't say anything for years. She started having nightmares from it. Then eventually started drinking to help cope with it. Things never got better because the last I heard, she had died from a drug overdose. Tiffany never answered my question so I thought I might have struck a nerve. I had to say something to let her know I was only trying to help.

"I mean, I've *heard* that sometimes things can happen in our past. Things that we don't always remember or even *want* to remember." Still, I heard nothing but I knew she was there. "Tiff, if you want me to come over so we can talk?"

Tiffany interrupts me so quickly I felt there must be more to the story than what she was telling me. "No, I got to start getting things ready for school tomorrow but we'll talk soon."

I didn't want our conversation to end this way. I also didn't want to push her into telling me what was wrong. "Okay, but call me if you need anything."

She said okay but I wanted her to know that I was totally sincere. "I mean it Tiff, if you need me for anything just call me and I'll come over."

"I know you will Q, but I'm good. I'll give you a call tomorrow."

λ THE DIARY λ
CHAPTER 11

Everything at school was going great. Only two more weeks before graduation and there was a party to go to every weekend. I even saw Tiffany at a few and she seems to be having a great time. Man, I'm going kinda miss this. Sean and I finally rode up to Georgia Tech. We checked out the campus and some other places too. It's going to be so much fun living in the ATL. You should have seen the smile on my mom's face when my graduation invitations arrived. With the money I'm making, things were starting to look up. Tiffany had invited me over for dinner and Ms. Alston roast beef was the bomb!

"So you and Sean are both going to Georgia Tech?"

I wasn't trying to be greedy but Ms. Alston had just asked if I wanted more and I couldn't resist. "Yes, Ma'am."

Ms. Alston sat the plate in front of me which was just a big as the first so I was about to go in. "Well, the bible says 'The Lord moves in mysterious ways with wonders to perform'. I'm proud of all of you, but I'm going to miss you guys. Especially my baby who's going *so* far away."

"We'll be coming home to visit Momma. Plus, that will give you a chance to get away sometime."

Tiffany had family that lived near Stanford but I couldn't imagine Ms. Alston going there much. But she kept telling Tiffany she wanted her to go to California because that's where she wants to retire someday.

"That's right, I haven't been to California in years but it's a beautiful place to live."

Well, I have never been California but if that's where Tiffany is going to be, I'll find a way to get there.

"So Quentin, are you guys having a graduation party?"

"No man, but we will definitely be at Tiffany's."

That's all Tiffany has been talking about for the past few days. Ms. Alston was throwing her a party at the Embassy Suite Downtown and Tiffany was so excited. She made sure to invite all of us, including Keyna even though she wasn't graduating. I heard that Keyna had moved over to View Side Manor to live with her sister. Now, let me tell you about View Side Manor, that place's rougher than over here. I've heard a four-year-old jacked another kid for a Tootsie Roll Pop, *while* the kid was still licking it! Well, I guess he'll never know how many licks it takes to get to the center of that Tootsie Roll Pop.

"Is there anything you need us to bring Ms. Alston?" Besides the cases of beer, some of my boys and I always sponsor at every occasion.

"Oh, no thank you Sweetie. You just make sure you guys are there."

My plans were already made to be there just in case Mr. Jemar tries to stop by. I wanted to ask Tiffany more about her and Jemar but her mom was right there. Is she really over that clown yet? I wonder what was going on in that pretty little head of hers.

Θ

Dear Diary,
IT's getting worst and IT seems
to have become my reality.
I try hard to control IT but now
feels like IT controlling me.
The face that I once didn't recognize,
IT's gotten clearer each time.
Why won't IT just go away?
before I lose my mind?

IT's getting harder to sleep at night
so I lay awake in fear.
Because even when I try to scream
no one else can hear.

71

I thought about what Quentin said
in remembering the past.
But IT makes no sense to me
and I'm too ashamed to ask.

I know the person in my dreams and
IT hurts to think it true.
And why should I tell anyone
if there's nothing they can do?
IT's getting worst and IT seems
to have become my reality.
I try hard to control IT but now
feels like IT controlling me.

With the summer almost here, I had some things lined up for the kids at the center. Okay, so the little Hood Pack was starting to grow on me. I promised them I would buy them pizza on Thursdays if they stopped hiding my keys, cell phone and please don't ask me how they got a hold of my watch. But with so much going on I haven't been running for EZ as much. People have been calling me day and night. Most of them wanted to buy from me. But right now, I got other things on my mind.

"So, you know we're supposed to ride with Jay Saturday night to check out that party? Yeah, I have this girl that's supposed to meet me there."

I was trying not to laugh at what Sean had just said. Sean had just started talking back to Leila, the same girl he'd like for the past two years. Leila would beat Sean down if he even thought about talking to another girl. "Oh, yeah most definitely."

We had just gotten to the Carver Community Center and a few of the boys and mentors were already there. Some of the kids were running up and down the court playing ball. The others were just hanging around talking or on their phones.

"Man, I can't believe we're moving. I posting a bunch of photos on my Instagram page."

Sean and I took a lot of shots while we were in Atlanta. He was more ecstatic about moving than I was. Yeah, I could remember when he first moved around here. Some skinny, little shy kid that got picked on a lot by some of the kids. His grandmother kind of help raised my mom, so she made me promise to look out for him.

"Hey Sean, you remember that time Steve Mullins and those boys wanted to beat you up?"

"How could I forget? We were in the sixth grade and them boys promised they were going to get us after school."

Sean started laughing. "Oh Yeah, I remember that. That

was the time you told them I was hiding in the janitor's closet, and when they went in we locked them in there for like two hours."

Now, Sean had me laughing. "Man, I never ran so fast before in my life when they got out. But the next day them boys whipped our ass!"

"Yeah, but we got in some good blows though! But you were always there for me Q, you're like my brother Man."

Wow, I could see that Sean was going to miss this place just as much as me. "Sean, how about the time we skipped class and snuck into the movies. Oh my God! We had so much fun back then. I use to tell my Mom I was going to the park to play ball and we would sneak off and go fishing."

"I remember that day we went fishing and Jarrod pushed me in that river."

I had no idea he couldn't swim until he started screaming. I jumped in without even thinking and pulled him out. All of the sudden Sean wasn't laughing anymore and I knew why.

"I would have drowned that day if you hadn't jumped in." Sean was looking down towards the gymnasium's floor. "You saved my life. I don't know how you did it but you."

I had to stop my man right there because I could see where this was going. The last thing I needed was to get emotional. Then some of these nappy headed kids see me crying. I'm sure at the next meeting they'll be bringing me some diapers and a baby bottle. "Man, you know I wasn't going to let anything happen to you. Like you said, we're brothers." I never told Sean that later that day I had to lie to my dad about how my new Nikes ended up in the dumpster.

"Q, you've always looked out for me, but from this day on, I promise I'm going to look out for you. We're about to head off to college!" Sean was back to his happy self again and everyone had started heading towards the bleachers for our meeting. "Q, I'm telling you. It's going to be so much fun living in the dorms together. We get to hang out whenever we want to."

"Yes! And we get to party whenever we want."

Sean and I started heading that way as well. Coach Barnes was still talking as we tried to lower our voice which wasn't hard over Couch Barnes' loud voice echoing across the gymnasium.

"Hitting all the campuses over there."

"Yes! And we get to party whenever we want."

Sean stopped and stared at me. "Q, you've already said

that."

"Yeah, I know."

Coach Barnes was talking about the upcoming trip in a few weeks to the Water Park. I had volunteered because I really wanted to go. Besides, I was too young to remember going to the Water Park before. Omar said he wanted to go too. So this would be a good time to get in some rides together before I left. Wow, I'm leaving The Aiken and this was not a dream. This was serious and now everything seemed for real.

λ STICC WAITING λ

CHAPTER 12

Riding the Malta Transit here was like playing with a loaded gun. But what can you do when that's the main transportation to get around? Most people here have been catching buses for years. So there's not much they haven't seen. Mr. Thomas had told us that he rather walk because the young folk now was just out of control. I mean everything from little kids cussing and swearing, to people having sex on there. Lately, to make things worse, they starting shooting on there. I'm telling you, it's getting crazier out here every day. Mr. Thomas was sitting in the park as usual when he saw Keyna getting off the bus.

"Well, I haven't seen you in a minute Keyna."

"Hey, Mr. T."

For the first time, Mr. Thomas didn't seem to be so annoyed by Keyna's loud mouth. "So, how have you been Keyna?"

"Well, you know I moved over to View Side Manor. But I'm here to see Mom and pick up a few stuff."

"And is that baby doing okay?"

"Yes, Sir." Keyna went over and sat next to Mr. Thomas. "I'm taking classes now to get my GED Mr. T."

"For Real? Well, I'm glad to hear that Keyna and I'm so proud of you."

"Well, you fussed at me enough about it."

Mr. Thomas smiled and nodded his head. "Yes, and it's about time you listened."

"Well, that's true. So what you out here waiting for?"

"My daughter and my grandkids are coming by to see me."

"Oh, I didn't know you had grandkids Mr. T."

"Yes, I have two grandkids and this would be my first time seeing them."

"Wow, well I hope you enjoy their visit. I'm going to the house and pick up some more things to take home." Keyna got up from the bench to leave. "Thanks, Mr. Thomas." Mr. Thomas has never heard Keyna called him that. She leaned over and kissed him on the forehead. "You've always been like the father I never had."

Now, I consider myself to be a pretty good judge of characters. For one, I know game when I see it because I'm a master at games. I promise you will learn quick growing up here. It's a game of survival to the finish! I can tell if someone was going to be a friend or my enemy. Without a doubt, Jemar was my enemy.

"I can't believe he's talking about me like that!"
I could understand why Tiffany was so upset. She needed to see Jemar for who he really was, *A Ho!* The word was out that he was telling people that he and Tiffany had slept together.

"No Sweetie, he's bragging about it. But you only have to give me the word and we'll see how well he plays with two broken legs."

"So he's going around lying on me?"

I'm assuming she was just hearing all of this for the first time.

"What else did he say?"

"Girl, you know me? That's grown folks' business so I don't get involved with stuff like that." I took another bite of some chicken salad which I helped myself to from Ms. Alston's fridge.

"Seriously Q?"

"You know Jemar is a Show-Off and is only trying to hurt you. So he's spreading rumors about you around school, on the football field, and even down at Tommy's Barber Shop." I felt the back of my head because I had just remembered what happened the last time I went to that barbershop. "Which by the way, don't *ever* send anybody there. His son Malcolm jacked up my cut so bad. Boy, I was mad cause he had my fad looking like a fag!"

Tiffany jumped up from the table and started pacing the floor. "You know what? That's it, I am so done with him and to think I was considering inviting him to my party."

"That's right, who he think he is? Girl, I'm just as mad as you are." Well, I wasn't as mad as I was happy knowing now that Jemar wasn't going to be there. But you know I had to pretend for Tiffany.

Tiffany stopped pacing and began talking again. This time she was moving her hands, which told me she had been around Keyna *way* too long. "See, that's what I'm talking about right there. That goes to show you, he doesn't care anything about me. Ever since he got that scholarship and that MVP award, he thinks every girl wants him."

"Yeah, and a few guys too." I'm sorry, but I had to throw that in there. I'm telling you he could go either way.

"Well, they all can have him." Tiffany sat back down and put her hand over her eyes and started crying. "I just don't know what to do anymore."

Wow, I wanted to bury Jemar but not at the expense of hurting Tiffany. "Listen Tiff, I'm sorry." I went to put my hand on her arm but then something unexpected happened, Tiffany turned and hugged me. It was only for a few seconds but it was the greatest hug I ever had. "So, you think you're going to be alright?"

Tiffany gave a slight smile as I tried to wipe a small tear from her eye. "Yes, I'm fine."

"I know you're fine as hell but are you going to be okay?"

Tiffany started laughing and then looked at me. "Yes, I'm going to be okay, but promise me you won't do anything to Jemar."

"Tiffany..." I was totally shocked! "What makes you think I would do anything to him?"

Tiffany looked me up and down. "Because I know you Q."

Damn! She might be right cause I had every intention on hurting him. Sure, Jemar had some punk ass varsity boys he hung with, but they were nothing compared to the crew I rolled with from The Aiken.

"What if I just *miss* and drop him off the top of a

building or something?"

Tiffany started laughing again. It was funny to me that she thought that was a joke. It would be so easy for Jemar to just trip and fall off a tall building.

"As much as I would like to kill him, he's not even worth it. So promise me you won't do anything."

"Okay… I promise I won't do anything to Jemar. So *now* do you feel better?"

There goes that beautiful smile. "I will feel better if we could finish off that lemon cake my mom left on the counter."

"See, that's what I'm talking about! Girl, you know how much I love your momma's lemon cakes."

Ms. Alston made the best cakes ever. Lemon, chocolate, strawberry it doesn't matter, cause it was all good. Besides, a brother needed to build up his appetite cause tomorrow I will be looking for Mr. Jemar. Yeah, I know I promised Tiffany I wouldn't touch him, but I definitely have a few friends who would.

λ LAST CHANCE λ

CHAPTER 13

I could hear my father yelling before I could get in the front door, which was a little surprising because it's usually me he's yelling at. Evidently, my father found out that Omar was getting high with his friends. Who would have thought he knew how to roll a joint. But my dad was going in! He wanted to know when he started smoking and who he got it from. I slowly walked across the living room hoping they wouldn't see me. I hadn't seen my dad that furious in years. For the most part, he's usually a calm mannered person. But right now, all calmness was gone. Omar was in tears but my father was not about to let up on his interrogation.

"This is the last time I'm going to ask you, Omar. Where did you get the weed from?"

Omar was trying his best to form some words together to answer my father. I could hardly make out what he was saying but I could hear my father loud and clear.

"And where did Blake get weed from?"

"From some guy named Mitch."

"Who in the hell is Mitch?"

My father may not know who Mitch was but I did. Mitchell K. Evans, some young snot head kid desperately trying to make a name for himself on the streets. My little brother was easily influenced and because of his disability was often taken advantage of.

"Dad, I'm sorry." His voice was soft and sincere and I felt sorry for him.

I was so caught up with everything I had going on I had let my guard down. I knew how these fools operated in The Aiken, and I knew my cousin had his part in it. I would be lying if I said I wasn't afraid to confront EZ, but this was my little brother.

"I want you home right after school from now on. No more going over to your friend's house or hanging out until I tell you to."

My father was totally serious. I remember he had me on lockdown for almost a whole month. My dad was so strict my friends use to call him The Warden. He use to threaten me, saying he promises if he kills me no one would miss me. *Now*, I knew he was only saying that to make me behave, and it worked!

"And if I *ever* see or hear anyone of you doing drugs, I will kill you myself." My father turned and glanced at me and at that moment I realized that he wasn't just saying it. *No*, my father was dead serious.

"I promise Dad, I'll never do it again." Omar was still crying but glad to be alive. Me, on the other hand, had to get myself together and quick. If you think he was pissed because Omar was smoking some weed, just imagine what he would do to me.

"And where have you been all day Quentin?"

He stared at me for a second but I had to think of something quick. "I…, well I'm just got off from work." Lord, please don't let him ask me anything else. I don't want to get caught in a lie because my Dad hears a lot of things on the streets.

"I'll talk with you in a minute."

Oh shit! I'm never going to get to graduate, I'm never going to make it to college. I'm not even going to get the chance to have no kids or anything. Maybe if I sneak out now I could make a run for it. I just stood there because I couldn't move. At least if he does kill me now I'll have a witness. That's unless he kills Omar too.

"You're grounded until you graduate high school."

Damn, that's like two years from now! Then my Dad started walking towards me. I was a little taller than him but he still put the fear of God in me. I've heard people say my dad use to bring down dudes twice his size.

"I need you to make sure to keep an eye on your brother." Man, I'm so glad that's what he wanted to talk about. "I'm not going to be here at nights cause I got a job down at the warehouse on Beaton Street."

I was happy my dad finally got a job but even happier that he hasn't found out about me hustling drugs. Right now I only needed a few more things to take care of and then I'm out of this game for good.

Something had to be seriously wrong for Ms. Alston to take a couple of days off from work. Whatever was going on she wasn't telling anyone. Tiffany was about to graduate and that was the only focus on her mind. Tiffany and I had just left the movies and we decided to stop by the STEAK N SHAKE before heading home.

"So you're saying you had nothing to do with Jemar and Josh getting jumped in the parking lot Tuesday?"

I had already started on my Double Chocolate Milk Shake and was getting a slight brain freeze. She had already asked me about this twice and again I told her 'No'.

"Why would I do something like that and jeopardize me getting suspended or something?" I wasn't sure if Tiffany was buying it or not. But that was my story and I was sticking to it.

"You know Q, I'm worried about my Mom."

"Well, what's going on with your Mom?"

"She's not telling me but I know something is wrong."

"Your mother is going to be fine, she's just nervous and everything because her baby is leaving home." I tried to convince Tiffany not to worry but that's easier said than done. "Have you thought any more about those dreams you've been having?" We had talked a little about it earlier but I was curious to what it all meant.

"Can I tell you a secret?"

Even my favorite burger I was devouring had lost my interest. Tiffany had never told me any of her secrets before. She could see she had my undivided attention.

"I know who the person is in my dreams." Tiffany was looking down at her plate. She had hardly touched her burger and was slowly chewing on one of her fries. I waited in anticipation for her to tell me but knew this couldn't be easy for her to talk about. "It's my brother."

Ms. Alston had Robert when she was very young. There was a huge age gap between him and Tiffany. He had left home a long time ago and I don't think anyone knew where he was.

"What, your brother Robert?" Tiffany didn't answer, she just picked up another fry and started chewing on it. "But why would you be having nightmares about him?"

Tiffany took a deep breath as let out a huge sigh. "Because he use to molest me when I was little."

Wow, I didn't even know how to respond to that. Evidently, Tiffany had blocked her brother out of her mind for a long time. "So, have you said anything to your Mom about it?"

I heard some kind of a laugh from Tiffany but knew from her expression it meant '*No*'. "Quentin, how can I tell my mother that my brother use to come into my room and molest me?"

Now it all was starting to make sense. The dreams, the nightmares and why Tiffany didn't want to say anything. "Tiff, you have to tell her."

Tiffany looked at me in disbelief. "I can't tell her right now Quentin. Whatever happened in the past I just have to deal with it. I'm not going to get my mother upset until I know how she's doing."

It was true that I was dealing with my own battles. I was too familiar with dealing with demons but not in my dreams. I couldn't allow Tiffany to fight them alone but who could I talk to without portraying her trust? "Tiffany, you can't go through this by yourself. Please just let me help."

I saw tears starting to well up in her eyes even though she fought back from crying. "Promise me Q that you won't tell anyone about this."

How could I make a promise like that now that I knew what her brother did to her? Now the nightmares that were possessing her dreams were now possessing me. I never imagined myself being a Demon Slayer but I was determined to help in any way possible. Maybe I could borrow my mother's bible or one of EZ's gun. I'm sure one or the other could take down a few demons.

λ CONFESSION λ

CHAPTER 14

Mr. Thomas had been waiting for years to see his daughter. Sabrina was very well dressed and drove a nice Acura MDX. I remember Mr. Thomas said she was an attorney, so I guess she's doing pretty good for herself. Mr. Thomas already had dinner and presents waiting. He had spent a lot of time and money hoping to make a good impression.

"So Sabrina, how's Aaron doing?

"He's doing great Daddy." Sabrina gave a huge sigh. "He's busy as usual so he couldn't make it for dinner."

Sabrina was playing with the rest of her food left on her plate. Mr. Thomas had put enough on the plates to last another meal. You could tell by her physique that she wasn't a big eater, and neither were the kids. They had left the table minutes ago to play with their new iPads.

"Maybe you all can come visit for a week or two this summer?" Mr. Thomas knew he probably was asking for too much but he had to make the offer.

"I don't think so Daddy. Both Aaron and I will be working plus the kids have camp in the summers."

"Well." Mr. Thomas paused trying to think of another possibility. He really wanted to spend more time with his son-in-law. They only had a brief encounter after the wedding ceremony. Aaron seemed to be a nice guy and was hoping to get to know him better. "How about you guys coming over for Thanksgiving or Christmas?"

"Daddy, we've already made plans to spend the holidays with Aaron's parents in Virginia." Sabrina sat there as she seems to be searching for the right words to say. "Listen Daddy, the only reason I came was because the kids were always asking about their grandfather. They get to see Aaron's side of the family all the time but never mine."

So that was the only reason she showed up? But Mr. Thomas already knew this but it hurt to hear it even more.

"Sabrina, what can I do to make things up to you?"

She could hear the sorrow in his voice but there was nothing he could do to change the past.

"Sweetheart, you have to understand I was very young when your mother and I got married. I knew I was going off to war but I had no idea the damage it would have caused." Mr. Thomas could see tears starting to fall from her eyes.

"There's no way I can make any excuses for the drinking and how abusive I was to your mother. I would give anything to have her here."

"But you can't!" Sabrina stared into her father's eyes. "So, I *don't* want to talk about it."

"I didn't want to tell you the truth, so for years I didn't say anything." Mr. Thomas sat up straight in his chair and took a deep breath as if it was his last. "Yes, I admit that I caused your Mother's death."

Sabrina interrupted him before he could say another word. "I said I don't want to talk about it."

Mr. Thomas wanted to get this out once and for all. He had held it inside for long enough. It was now or never! "Your mother did everything one woman could have done to keep our family together. Even when her mother and friends begged her to leave, she still stayed." Mr. Thomas cleared his throat as if the words were caught there and didn't want to come out. "Your mother stayed because she was pregnant with your brother."

Sabrina burst out in tears but Mr. Thomas couldn't move, not even to console his daughter. He had to finish telling her the truth. "Your mother died while giving birth to our son."

Mr. Thomas sat there waiting for Sabrina to say something, *anything*! Sabrina was finally able to stop crying. Now she was even more confused. "So why didn't you tell me this before?"

"Because I didn't want you to hate me, just like you do right now. That's why I kept you away from everybody. I was ashamed and I didn't want to lose you too."

"And for what? So by you confessing to me now is supposed to change anything?"

Mr. Thomas shook his head because he knew she was right. A small tear started to form in his eyes as he tried to continue. "I'm so sorry Sabrina."

"So even though you knew she was pregnant, you didn't change?"

"But I changed because of you Sabrina; you were all I had left. I have no one, do you understand?"

Sabrina stood up as her eyes searched the room for her pause. "I have to go." Mr. Thomas stood up as well but knew there was nothing he could do or say to keep her from leaving. Sabrina yelled for the kids in the other room. "AJ and Erica let's go!" The kids came from out the bedroom but their eyes were still glued to their iPads.

"Sweetheart, I know you're still upset with me. Please, if you can find a way to forgive me."

"I got to go." Sabrina grabbed her purse and headed towards the front door. The kids started mumbling under their breath that they weren't ready yet. "And don't forget to thank your grandfather for the gifts!"

The kids went over to hug their grandfather and said 'Thanks Granddaddy'. Mr. Thomas held back tears while wishing he never had to let them go. *'Granddaddy'*. But this may be the first and last time he'll ever see them. Mr. Thomas followed them to the door as Sabrina and the kids headed towards the car. Sabrina stopped and turned towards her father. "Goodbye Daddy."

I wondered what life would have been like if we didn't live in The Aikens? I think it would have been a little easier but boring. *Here*, there is never a dull moment. Tatianna passed me on my way to the Boys Club. Tatianna lived on the next block and always spoke. She would call me 'Cutie' and said she wish I was older so I could be her boyfriend. Tatianna had a beer can in one hand while smoking a black and mild and talking on the phone with the other. I still don't know how she does that without burning herself.

I could hear Mr. Phillip across the street carrying on a whole conversation with *himself.* "I already told you, you can't have any more Monty."

Now, if I didn't know any better, I would have sworn he was talking to at least *three* other people. Monty, Tony and Kym. Just last week he was fussing at his imaginary dog, Ham Bone. Ham Bone evidently took his sandwich without asking and Mr. Phillip was mad as hell. My dad said he believed someone gave him some bad dope. Mr. Phillip hasn't been the same ever since. That's why you can't trust a lot of people anymore.

"If you ask me that *one* more time, I'm going to kill you!" Okay... I'm not too sure how crazy Mr. Phillip was but I'm glad I'm headed in the opposite direction.

"What's up King?" Now, I haven't seen this dude in a long time. Kevin rarely came over to this side of the neighborhood anymore.

"What's up Big Q?" Kevin had a huge smile on his face as he gave me dab. "What have you been up to?"

"Not much King, I heard you're going to be the DJ at Tiffany's party?"

"Yeah, you know I'm going to be up in there."

King was a little cocky but he was cool though. I always thought his head was a little too big for his body. I guess that's why he always walk with a little lean on the side.

"Have you seen Keyna lately?"

Now that you asked, I haven't seen her in a while. "No I haven't seen her either." Like if I did I would tell him. Keyna would have told him where she was if she wanted him to know.

"Well, she'll probably be at that party. I doubt if she would miss that."

"Yeah, that's true."

"If you happen to see her, let her know I asked about her."

"Sure deal King."

Keyna might be done with him for good this time. It's kinda sad cause he really does love that baby. But you can't be a man and still doing childish things. Maybe Sean has the right idea about helping to make a difference here. Even though those kids at the Boys Club were bad as hell, they're starting to grow on me.

λ WHAT'S NEXT λ

CHAPTER 15

Less than a week before graduation and the seniors were extra hyped! A lot of them didn't make it into a college. Hell, most of them barely made it out of high school. But to have two of my closest friends get into a college was something to celebrate. This was our year and we were about to *Turn Up*!

"So, is your Aunt Andrea going to be able to make it to the graduation?" Sean wanted to know because he was hoping his daughter Shamel was coming with her.

"Oh yeah, she said she can't wait to see me walk across that stage. Plus she said she had a little something for me too."

"For real! So is your cousin Shamel coming too?"

"No Sean. She has a job now so she can't make it."

I was clearing the rest of my things out of my locker. An old soda can, lots of undone homework, and some gum that must have been there from the year before that I refuse to touch.

"Besides, didn't Shamel beat you up the last time she was here?"

Sean sucked his teeth and shook his head. "She didn't beat me up, she was just playing with me."

"Then why did I have to come and get her off of you?"

Sean never was much of a fighter and I had to keep reminding him of that. But right now we had a lot to do and a short time to do it in. I pulled out a magic marker that was in the back of the locker. Wow! After all this time it still worked.

"Man Q, what are you writing?"

I thought it would be nice to leave a message for all of those we were leaving behind and it read SO LONG SUCKERS!!!

My dad was starting to ask too many questions about the things I was buying. I was trying my best to keep a low profile but that's almost impossible to do around here. I needed to talk to EZ. If my dad found out that EZ was the one supplying Mitch with the drugs Omar was using, there was going to be *Hell* to pay! EZ was late as usual, but when he drove up he was on his phone yelling at somebody.

"You tell that Bitch that when I see him he better have my money!" Anyone who knew EZ knew he didn't play when it came to money. "Well tell him I'm looking for his bitch ass."

I walked over to the car and EZ looked up at me.

"Just hold tight, I'll be with you in a minute."
'Man, you can take all the time you want.' I wasn't trying to upset him any more than he already was. EZ stepped out the car still cussing while searching through his numbers.

"What up Q, you needed to talk? Make it quick cause I got something to do."

"Yeah, I got this for you." I passed him a package some dude name Floyd gave me just 15 minutes ago.

"Okay, thanks Man." EZ didn't even look to see what was inside. But my guess was that he already knew.

"Listen EZ, I know I can't tell you how to run your business. But my dad found out your boy Mitch was selling drugs to Omar."

"Mitch! That punk ass bitch doesn't work for me anymore. He's mad because I'm paying you more than him."

EZ was still talking but now I'm totally confused about

what was going on. I was under the impressing that Mitch was still working for EZ. I didn't realize Sean was approaching until I saw EZ looking pass my shoulder.

"Hey, what's up Sean?" EZ said it loud enough to inform me Sean was walking towards us. But Sean was smart enough to know, that whenever EZ was around, it wasn't good. Sean walked up with a look of disbelief so I'm sure he overheard part of our conversation.

"What's up with me? No Q, what's up with you?" Sean had a serious frown on his face as he looking EZ up and down. "You mean to tell me, you got my man out here hustling for you?"

EZ was just as shock as I was to hear Sean talk like that. Sean was usually the quiet one and I was the one always getting into fights. "Listen! I don't have him out here doing nothing. Q came asking me for help, so what now?"

"Hey Sean, me and my cousin just talking about a few things."

"Well you know you're wrong Q."

"Well you know you're wrong Q." EZ repeated what Sean said mocking him. "Yeah, you know what's wrong Sean? You being here, so why don't you leave and go read a book or something."

"No, you need to stop trying to make him like you."

"Nigga please, don't you understand he's just like me! How else do you think we're going to get anything out of this trap?"

"Listen Sean, just stay out of this. This is between me and my cousin."

"So what now Q? You got accepted into college. You just need to apply for some more grants. You don't need to be out here doing this."

EZ started laughing but Sean was straight serious. "Grants! I got your Grants *and* your Benjamins." He pulled out a roll of money held together by a rubber band. Man, with this kind of money, I could just pay somebody to go to college for me. "This is all the education I need, my personal funds from The Black Ghetto United Trust."

I watched as my cousin walked back into his car and drove off.

"Man are you crazy? How could you do something like this?"

Something like this? Sean was clueless to what I was dealing with. "Sean, you don't know how hard things have been. So don't you tell me what I should or shouldn't do! You're not the one who had to listen to your mother cry at night cause she didn't know how the mortgage was going to get paid. Or if the lights were going to get turned off or not."

"Listen Q, I know it's not easy."

"You don't know nothing! Just a few months ago I was stealing hot dogs from work because I didn't want my little sister or brother going to bed hungry. And I promised myself, I'll do whatever it takes to make sure they had food and a roof over their head. So, you *don't* know what I've been going through so just leave me the hell alone!"

As my best friend, I could understand where Sean was coming from. He was like my brother and we always had each other's back.

"Q…, I'm sorry. I swear I didn't know."

Sean didn't know because I never said anything. I guess I was too embarrassed to tell anyone. Maybe I shouldn't have said those things. At least I still had a mother, Sean didn't. I couldn't even imagine my mother not being there when I walked across the stage. I just needed to get away and be by myself for a minute. "I got to get out of here; I'll talk to you later."

"No problem Man."

We heard music approaching in the distance and someone pulled up in a silver GMC Envoy. I still had a few ounces and was going to give them whatever I had. I'm through with this and just wanted out!

"Hey, where's EZ?" You got to be shitting me! It was Mitch with two other guys riding with him.

"He left but I need to talk to holla at you a minute."

I heard the guy on the passenger side said something but couldn't make it out. Besides, it didn't really matter. This was between Mitch and me.

"You're EZ's cousin right?"

"Yeah."

"Well, I got a message for him."

I swore I didn't see a gun and before I knew it, Mitch had started firing shots in our direction. "Look out Sean!" Was the only thing I could think to say as we both dropped to the ground. I heard the car spun off and yelled at Sean to just stay down. My heart was beating so fast. I couldn't believe this fool just shot at me! "Are you alright Sean?"

Mitch had no idea what he just started. Nobody takes shots at me and gets away with it. I'm going to unload a whole clip into him when I catch him. Then I realized that Sean never responded to me. "Sean, you okay man?" I looked over to where Sean was lying. *'Why isn't he answering me?'* Maybe he's just too scared or maybe he hurt himself. I knew we hit the concert pretty hard but he needs to say something. "Sean!" I jumped up and hurry over to make sure Sean was okay. He was faced down and I could see blood streaming from beneath him. He wasn't breathing. *'He wasn't breathing.'*

"Sean, come on man. *Please*, please don't die man."

Please Sean, you can't leave, not now. I turned him over and there was so much blood. I held his head up while trying to remember the CPR Course we took at the Boys Club. But I couldn't remember anything, I couldn't even think. Then I realized that Sean was gone. But that can't be possible!

"Oh my God, what happened?" I heard voices but couldn't tell you who they were. People had heard the shots and ran out to see what had happened. Then I heard someone yelled to call the EMS and people screaming and crying. I was crying too. I had cried so hard by this time that I could barely speak. I just wasn't ready to let go. "Please, don't leave me Sean. Please, I'm begging you."

λ 1FEVER AGAIN λ

CHAPTER 16

Nothing has been the same since that day Sean died. Graduation day was now nothing to be excited about anymore. Even Tiffany canceled her party because she couldn't go through with it. It was supposed to be a celebrating with all four of us there. We walked across the auditorium stage and received our degrees but it didn't seem to matter that much. Nothing really matters anymore! It was just a piece of paper that only meant we survived high school. *So what!* We needed to survive life and that seemed almost impossible. Sean should have been here, he deserved this more than I did. Hell, if it wasn't for him I probably wouldn't have graduated. He was the smart one; he was the one who motived me to even think about college.

"Q, I'm telling you I got this."

Trying to convince me to stay out was not going to work. EZ was promising me that he was going to take care of everything. This was Sean, not only was he my best friend but he was my brother. "I'm not leaving until I see his brain splattered on the concrete."

"And I understand Lil' Cuz. But you've finally got a chance to get out of here. Let me just handle this."

Maybe EZ was right and I am just like him. The only thing on my mind was to get Mitch back for what he did to Sean. EZ knew that Mitch was looking to take him out so the word on the street was that EZ was coming for him. So what if we got caught and I ended up in prison? 'You take out one of mine, then I'm going to take out one of yours.' That's just how we do it in The Aiken.

"Mitch has probably left town by now. Do you think the cops are going to be searching for him like that? As far as their concern Sean is just one less young Nigga they have to worry about."

I knew a few brothers that gotten killed over the years and the killers never got convicted. But that wasn't going to happen with Sean. I was going to make sure Mitch paid for this shit!

"Have I *ever* lied to you before Lil' Cuz?"

Wow, now that I think about it, EZ has never lied to me. He has done a lot of crazy shit and I went along because I was a badass little boy myself. My father thought EZ was a bad influence but most of that stuff I would have done anyway.

"No EZ, you've always been straight with me."

"Okay, then trust me when I tell you I got this. He was out to get me so there's nowhere he can hide."

Now the Hunted has become the Hunter. Mitch better pray that the police got hold of him before EZ did. I was still confused, how can I just sit around and do nothing? But I also know that if I went after Mitch, I can forget leaving for college. I know I don't ask for much from anybody, but *'Lord I am asking you to help me get through this.'*

The park seems empty as ever. I could hear some kids laughing and playing on the swings. Suddenly I remembered when that use to be me. Life was so much simpler and I wished I could go back, if only for a moment. I remembered the first day I met Sean. He was at this park holding his Spaulding basketball which at the time seemed too big for his hands. I asked him if he wanted to play a little one on one and we played ball together ever since. I hope no one could see me crying but this hurts more than anything I've ever known.

"Hey Sean, I still can't believe you're gone. Aiken Park sure ain't going to be the same without you. I knew you said you'll look out for me, so I hope you can hear me now. Listen, I'm sorry for yelling at you and everything. Please forgive me Man; you know I didn't mean any of that stuff. Hey listen! Your grandmother gave me your favorite basketball so I hope you don't mind."

For some reason, I couldn't explain but I had brought the

109

ball with me. I knew Sean won't mind me having it because he said I could use it whenever I liked. In a strange way, I was hoping he would be here so we could play ball together. I looked up towards heaven praying that he could hear me.

"I also wanted to tell you that I decided to still go to Georgia Tech, and thank you for staying on me. I promise I won't let you down and you're going to be so proud of me. I just want you to know that I love you, Man. And if ever again, I pray to have the chance to see you. I want to let you know that you'll always be my brother."

"Hey, are you okay Quentin?

I'm not sure how long Tiffany was standing there and didn't care. I was just happy she was here. "Yeah, I'm straight." I promised myself not to let anyone see me cry, but that was easier said than done. "How about you, are you doing alright?"

Tiffany sat down beside me but was still looking in the distant. Not for anything in particular but more of a wandering glare. "I'm feeling okay. I was trying to call you earlier."

I pulled my phone out and realized I hadn't turned it back on since last night. Mostly, people were calling wanting to know what happened. Others, just looking to score some drugs. Either way, I was tired and didn't want to be bothered.

"Sean is dead and it's because of me Tiffany." Tears started flowing down my face again because I know that if I had never contacted EZ, none of this would have happened.

"Q, what happened was not your fault."

But how could I bring myself to tell Tiffany everything and if I did, would she ever see me the same way again?

"Yes, it was my fault cause that guy was looking for EZ that night. That bullet was meant for me because I was EZ's cousin. So, I could have taken that shot, not Sean!" I couldn't stop myself from crying. Sean was lying in a casket because I allowed myself to get involved with the wrong people.

"Q, they're going to get the guy who did this and he's going to go to prison."

Did she just say *Prison*? "No Tiffany, I want Mitch dead!"

"I can't imagine how you feel Quentin, but that's not going to bring Sean back. He would have wanted you to go out there and have the best life possible. And maybe we can even come back one day and help make things a little better for others."

As much as I hate to admit it, that is exactly what Sean would have wanted. I was so great with the Boys Club. The kids had even created a nice memorial in his honor at the center.

"But we were supposed to do this together. I don't know if I can do this by myself."

"Yes you can Q, I didn't think there's anything you can't do."

Wow, that would have been something Sean would say.

"So, are you going to be alright?"

This was the first time anyone made me smile since Sean's death. "Yeah, I'm good."

Tiffany leaned over and placed her head on my shoulder and spoke in her soft lovely voice. "That's my Q." We both lost track of time as we sat there laughing and reminiscing. We talked about all the great times the four of us had together. It was starting to get dark so I offered Tiffany to walk her home.

"Thanks, Quentin." Tiffany had stopped for a moment before heading towards her door.

"What for?" Because I couldn't imagine what in the

world she would need to thank me for. If anything, I needed to be thanking her.

"For being my best friend."

I could see a smile on that pretty face as she walked away and went inside. *'Wow, her best friend!'* I repeated to myself in my mind. I wasn't expecting her to say that, so who knows what the future might hold. Of course, I would love to be more than just her best friend, but I'll take that for now.

In loving memories of my son Jacob and many others who lives were snatched away at such a young age.

Θ

ANOTHER CHILD IS GONE

I must go far away from here
To a place where there are no more tears
Time has come; don't want to leave this way
Don't want to leave you now, but I can not stay
Another child is born
Another child is gone
Can't see another day
To never come back home

Lord, I know you take the best for you
But in this place, what are we going to do?
And Lord, you know what's right and what's wrong
But please tell me why another child is gone?
Another child is born
Another child is gone
To never walk this way
So please come back home

Tyre' Gadsden moved from Charleston to Atlanta after the loss of her son Jacob. Tyre' comes from a close and large family who encouraged her to become a writer. She has two other children Quawnta Snow and Scott Snow. Also 3 grandsons Keondre, Devonte and Romeo. Tyre' created South Kingdom Productions to assist young actors and artists to develop and showcase their talent. Tyre' loves to travel and spending time on the beach, cooking, decorating, and most of all she loves to entertain. Tyre' performed as a lead singer and musician for several years and afterward wrote her first stage play '*CAN ANYTHING GOOD COME OUT THE HOOD*?'. Now the book and play have become a Sitcom with many more incredible shows to follow.